CW00421184

Marrying Mr. Darcy: A Sensual "Pride & Prejudice" Variation

Abbey North

Published by Abbey North JAFF Books, 2022.

This is a work of fiction. Similarities to real people, places, or events are entirely coincidental.

MARRYING MR. DARCY: A SENSUAL "PRIDE & PREJUDICE" VARIATION

First edition. October 29, 2022.

Copyright © 2022 Abbey North.

ISBN: 979-8215868782

Written by Abbey North.

Blurb

Someone is marrying Mr. Darcy, but which one?

EIGHTEEN YEARS AGO, Fitzwilliam left Netherfield and Lizzy behind after they nearly shared a kiss. Lizzy couldn't dwell on the knowledge he was going to marry Anne, because she had to accept Mr. Collins' proposal after her father's untimely death. She consigned her feelings for Fitzwilliam to a deep place in her mind, never to be considered.

Years later, her daughter returns home from a visit to Rosings Park with the news William Darcy wants to marry her. Lizzy is at first opposed to her daughter marrying Mr. Darcy's son, but after seeing them together, she's convinced Lottie will be happy with the boy. It's no surprise when Mr. Darcy appears in full wrath, intent on preventing the union. As Lizzy and Fitzwilliam clash about their children's futures, the past they never addressed lingers between them. Will passions ignite and give them a second chance, or are they both too proud and prejudiced to embrace this new opportunity?

This features a widely divergent timeline sprinkled with a dash of what-if. What if a reformed Lady Catherine, shaped by grief, has mellowed and wants to play matchmaker? What if Lizzy took the reins of Longbourn? What if Fitzwilliam never learned to temper his pride in the past and is forced to do so now to embrace a chance at a happy future?

ABBEY NORTH

While Abbey sometimes writes sweet JAFF, this is strictly SENSUAL.

Prologue

THE NEWS FROM NETHERFIELD was terrible. Lizzy had barely begun her morning walk when she ran into servants from the adjoining property. They'd informed her the occupants of Netherfield were packing up and leaving. Mr. Bingley had gone on earlier, and Lizzy imagined Mr. Darcy had been with him. Thinking of the man sent a pang through her chest, and she couldn't help recalling just the night before, when she had danced with him. He wasn't much of a conversationalist, but there had been a moment when their eyes met as they were completing a complicated dance step, and she had sworn he was going to kiss her.

Of course, that would've caused a great scandal and ruined her unless he offered marriage quickly thereafter, which she was under no illusion he would do. After all, according to Mr. Collins, he was already betrothed to Anne de Bourgh, so he wasn't free to pursue any feelings he might have for Lizzy anyway. Perhaps that was what had prompted his departure from Netherfield, but it seemed unnecessarily cruel that he was also taking Mr. Bingley with him. After all, Mr. Bingley had great fondness for Jane, or seemed to, and Lizzy knew her sister loved him. Jane was bound to be devastated when she heard the news.

As though thinking of her sister had conjured her, Jane came running from the house, waving to catch Lizzy's attention. At first, she assumed Jane must have heard the news the Netherfield party was departing, because her sister's face was bright red, and her eyes were blotchy. Tears stained her cheeks, and it was obvious she'd been crying. As soon as Jane caught up with her, Lizzy said, "Oh, dear sister, all hope is not lost."

Jane blinked, looking surprised for a second. "I know not of what you speak, but you must come quickly." She was tugging inelegantly at Lizzy's arm as she spoke.

Her sheer desperation seemed to be far out of proportion to the news of Mr. Bingley leaving Netherfield, which caught Lizzy's full attention. "What troubles you, Jane?"

"Oh, it is terrible, Lizzy. Papa has collapsed in his library."

Lizzy gathered her skirts and ran after her sister, soon overtaking Jane in her haste. Her heart was beating a frantic signal in her chest, and it felt like she couldn't draw in a deep breath as fear washed over her. She couldn't lose her dear papa.

She burst into the house, darting out of the range of Mr. Collins, who seemed to be waiting with an expression of concern. He probably meant well, but she had no time for him right then.

She ran down the hall and burst into the library, finding it empty. "Where...?" She let out several deep gasps as she tried to regain control of her breathing.

"He has been moved upstairs, Miss Eliza," said Mr. Collins in a solicitous tone. "It would be my honor to escort you."

She nodded, but she didn't really wait for him. She turned and raced up the stairs, uncaring it was not ladylike in the least. The sheer urgency of Jane's summons suggested it was more than something trivial plaguing her father.

When she burst in, Mr. Jones was standing over her father, who looked pale. Pale didn't even begin to adequately describe him, quite truthfully. He was whiter than the white linen he laid against, practically gray in places, with large shadows under his eyes. He looked like he had aged twenty years in a day, and she rushed to his side, taking his hand. "Oh, Papa, what troubles you?"

"I do not believe he can speak," said Mrs. Bennet. "Oh, my nerves. Why must you do this to my nerves, Mr. Bennet?"

Her father's lips twitched slightly, and he managed to open his eyes. "Chose not to speak." Those words obviously cost him a great deal. "Was waiting." He gave Lizzy a significant look. "Love you, my daughter. Love you all." He closed his eyes again.

Lizzy clutched his hand tighter. "Papa, what is it? What can we do?"

"I am afraid there is nothing to be done, Miss Bennet," said Mr. Jones. The apothecary wore an expression of grief. "Your father's heart is barely beating, and it is only a matter of time until it gives out."

"Oh, he mentioned chest pains last night, but I insisted that he must come with us to the ball. Do you remember, Mr. Collins?"

Lizzy stiffened slightly at the idea of the man standing in the room where her father was slowly dying. He truly had no right to be there, though he was technically family. For a moment, all her rage and helplessness at the situation wanted to direct to Mr. Collins. It took every ounce of control not to turn and scream at the man to get out.

Her father's hand tightening slightly on hers helped her regain focus on what was important, and as his eyes opened again, she leaned closer. "What is it, Papa?"

"I am sorry, Lizzy." He had a little more strength in his tone. "I planned poorly for all of you, and I fear you must now pay the price for everyone. Think long and hard about the choice you make when it is offered to you, my girl. I would never have you marry for anything but love, but I do not think you have that luxury now."

Lizzy's head whirled with confusion as she leaned back, and when Mr. Collins put a hand on her shoulder, she froze in dismay while thinking about shrugging it off.

Fanny rushed forward to sit by Thomas, taking his other hand. He whispered something to her, and whatever it was, it must have been lovely, because her mother smiled for a moment before she burst into tears again. "Oh, my nerves. What will I do without you, my dearest Thomas?"

Lizzy eased back, allowing all her sisters a chance to say their goodbyes. Mr. Jones seemed so dour about the possibility that they would have much more time, and she refused to be selfish enough not to allow them all to say something. Even Lydia pushed forward, presenting a great deal of theatricality as she threw herself against Papa and wept. Lizzy imagined the emotion was genuine, but her younger sisters tended to be overly dramatic.

She sat quietly, lost in a fog of grief as the others said their goodbyes. When she was satisfied they'd had time with him, she moved closer again, realizing Mr. Collins had kept his hand on her shoulder the entire time. She took her father's hand in hers, and his gaze met hers. He gave her a small smile before he breathed his last. With his final exhalation, his words sank into her mind, and she was then able to grasp them.

He referred to the forthcoming and unwanted proposal from Mr. Collins. Lizzy had braced herself to reject him, expecting an ugly scene, but in light of the death of her father, she understood what he had meant when he said she no longer had the luxury of declining. Papa hadn't phrased it quite that way, but she'd gotten the message. If she wanted to take care of her mother and sisters and herself, to save her home, she would have to undertake the unpleasant task of becoming Mrs. William Collins.

She wasn't certain whether it was the grief of losing her father or the knowledge of losing her future, but suddenly, the floodgates burst, and she let out a small wail and drew into herself, barely aware of Jane and her other sisters coming to embrace her a second later. She heard Fanny telling Mr. Collins to give them some time, but she wasn't really paying attention to that. She was grateful for the reprieve, no matter how slight, but she couldn't stave off the inevitable forever. After a suitable period of mourning, she would be forced to accept Mr. Collins' proposal.

Chapter One

EIGHTEEN YEARS LATER

Lizzy waited impatiently for the barouche box bearing the de Bourgh family crest to arrive at the end of the Longbourn drive. It had been a long visit, and she'd missed Lottie terribly during the six weeks her daughter had been gone. It was all she could do not to call out to the driver impatiently to speed up as he crossed the last hundred meters between the road and her.

She didn't even wait for the driver to get down. She burst forward and opened the door, allowing her daughter to step out before she embraced her. Lizzy took a step back, admiring her pretty features and naturally curly hair. Fortunately for Lottie, she'd inherited nothing from Mr. Collins save for the light color of his eyes and the slightly large shape of his ears.

That was easily hidden with hair, and she never failed to think how beautiful her daughter was and how lucky she was to have been blessed with Lottie. That and saving Longbourn had been the only two true good things that came out of her short marriage to Mr. Collins.

She almost laughed at herself. Even all these years later, she could barely bring herself to think of him as William, and she didn't think she'd ever called him William during the brief duration of their marriage. Even in the marriage bed, if she had addressed him at all, she was certain she'd used Mr. Collins.

She shook her head as she had the thought, realizing it was out of place under the circumstances. "You look beautiful, my dear. How was your visit with Lady Catherine?"

"She is a dear old thing, and I had a wonderful time, but best of all, William was visiting."

Lizzy's mouth became dry at the thought. "William Darcy?" It must be him, the son of Fitzwilliam Darcy and Anne de Bourgh. Having lost his mother at birth, he often spent time at Rosings Park among his other relations though often without his father. Lizzy wasn't certain she approved of that, but it wasn't her place to approve or disapprove of Mr. Darcy's raising of his only son.

"He was visiting before going to Cambridge this autumn. He shall live in London in a fine apartment, and it is the very one his father lived in along with a Mr. Wickham. I do not know the man, but his name came up a couple of times when William was speaking of Cambridge. William said his father does not seem to like mentioning Mr. Wickham."

"I can hardly be surprised at that. Mr. Wickham was not of good moral character."

That had been well-proven when the scoundrel had inadvertently ruined Charlotte after hearing a rumor Sir Lucas was quite wealthy. He'd gone after Charlotte relentlessly, but her friend was too practical to fall for the man's schemes and lies, so Wickham had orchestrated to be caught alone with her, forcing a marriage. It was only upon learning he'd been misinformed of her fortune that he had departed in the middle of the night before the wedding could take place.

After the scoundrel had absconded from Meryton, Charlotte's reputation had been ruined, and any faint remaining prospects of marriage had faded entirely. It had been more than poor Charlotte could stand, and she'd faded away and died within half a year. Ostensibly it had been from pneumonia, but Lizzy couldn't help thinking it had more to do with a broken heart at her tarnished reputation.

"It is most exciting, Mama." Lottie looked like she could barely contain herself. "Oh, I suppose I should not tell you yet, but I cannot wait." With a squeal of excitement, she said, "William is coming to visit us at Longbourn, and while he is here, he will ask for my hand in marriage."

Lizzy's eyes widened, and her mouth dropped open in shock. "You are but seventeen."

"It does not matter. I know I love him. Aunt Lydia married the brother of Harriet Forster when she was but sixteen. Kitty was only seventeen when she married Uncle Fields. They are both still happy, are they not?"

Lizzy could hardly deny that. Her younger sisters had been luckier in marriage than Lizzy had been, both still happily married to this day. Even Mary had spent a few happy years with her law clerk before he died suddenly, and she'd returned to living at Longbourn.

Jane was perhaps the happiest of all the sisters and had been for many years. When Mr. Bingley had returned the next spring for hunting after his hasty departure the autumn before, he had renewed his romance with Jane, having previously believed she had no interest in him. He hadn't known their father had died, and there had been no chance to travel or even write letters for a time.

His offer of marriage had been well timed for Jane, but it had been poor timing for Lizzy, for she'd already been married to Mr. Collins for two weeks by then. Had she known there was an option or a possibility of something else, she never would've accepted the proposal.

At least she'd had the good fortune for him to get himself killed in a plowing accident shortly after his takeover of Longbourn. She felt a small pang of sadness for his ill fate, because he hadn't been a cruel man. He'd just been oafish and obsequious, and there had been absolutely nothing about him that she loved. Lizzy had tried, but she hadn't been able to get past her repugnance of his character, and their blatant mismatch as a couple.

They had spent four months living at the rectory first before returning to Longbourn, because it had taken that long to settle his affairs and to find his replacement. During that time, Lizzy had met the infamous Lady Catherine de Bourgh. She'd fully anticipated disliking the woman, having heard so much about her from Mr. Collins. To her surprise, Lady Catherine had been loud and a bit overbearing, but she'd also shown hints of kindness.

Lizzy had stood up for herself on more than one occasion, such as resisting putting shelving in the rectory closets, which seemed to have impressed Catherine with her backbone rather than put her off. Oh, Catherine still chastised her about her impertinent opinions to this day, but they had gotten close during those four months, and it had been a surprising turn of events when Lady Catherine showed up and stayed as a guest for two months at Longbourn following Mr. Collins' untimely death.

Lizzy had been pregnant with Lottie by then, and Catherine had been anticipating the arrival of her own grandchild. For Lizzy, her story had ended happily enough. Being married to Mr. Collins for five months and being courted for several months before that had been plenty of time spent in his company. She had Lottie and control of Longbourn to show for the experience, and that was certainly well worth everything she'd had to endure for less than a year. She'd also formed that surprising friendship with Lady Catherine, who was still somewhat like a grandmother to Lottie.

Oddly enough, Lizzy wondered for second what Lady Catherine would've thought of her if she had perceived her as a rival for Mr. Darcy's affections back then. Of course, the near kiss had never been mentioned to anyone, and for all Lizzy knew, it was all in her mind. She was embarrassed to consider it again all these years later, but it was no mystery why she was thinking of Mr. Darcy today, since his son was due to arrive soon to ask for her daughter's hand in marriage.

Her first instinct was to protest and say an immediate no. "You are so young, daughter. I do not know that it is a good idea to marry so early in spite of Kitty and Lydia's successes. I was nearly one-and-twenty when I got married, and I still did not feel completely prepared." That had more to do with the identity of her groom than her age, but she wasn't going to reveal that about her daughter's father. She'd done her best to ensure Lottie had only good information about her father, feeling she owed Mr. Collins that, since he'd tried to be a good husband and probably could have been for the right wife. Lizzy just hadn't been the right one.

"I am most sure that I love him, and I do ask for your blessing, Mama. Officially, I know Uncle Bingley will have to give his blessing, but I could never go through with it without your blessing as well."

"If you are that certain, how can I deny you a chance at happiness?" She still had her reservations, chief among them her daughter's age, but also the fact that she was about to tie herself to a Darcy. Lizzy wondered if Fitzwilliam Darcy had yet received the news that his son planned to marry so beneath him. Perhaps once Mr. Darcy discovered the plan, he would put quietus to it before William could ever appear to ask for Lottie's hand.

She clung to that hope as she followed her daughter into the house. She didn't want to deny her daughter a chance to follow her heart, but she seemed so young, and Lizzy didn't even know the young man in question, not having seen him since he was four years old. It might be best if their fledgling romance died before it could develop any further.

Almost bouncing with excitement, it was obvious Lottie was anxious to greet the servants and Fanny after having been gone so long. They were dining with the Bingleys that evening, so Lottie would have a chance to catch up with her six cousins, and Lizzy could speak to Jane and Charles privately about the forthcoming proposal, if it actually occurred.

WHEN LIZZY MET WILLIAM Darcy the next day, he was far too much like his father for her comfort for a long instant. She stared at him, mouth agape, and it was almost like being eighteen years in the past, though William was younger than his father had been then. He had Mr. Darcy's dark hair and brown eyes, though his lips were fuller than she recalled his father's being. She blinked when she realized she had waited a half-second too long to respond to Lottie's introductions. "Hello, Mr. Darcy. It is lovely to see you. I have heard much about you." That was the truth, for Lottie could scarcely stop talking about her beau.

He kissed her glove and bent forward respectfully for a moment. "It is wonderful to meet you, Mrs. Collins."

She smiled. "I have actually met you once before, Master...Mr. Darcy. I was visiting Lady Catherine at Rosings Park when you and Lottie were about four. I believe you were accompanying your Aunt

Georgiana and her husband. You have changed quite a lot," she added with a gentle smile.

He grinned. "I do not remember that, but one of my earliest memories is chasing Lottie among the roses at Lady Catherine's home." He looked at her daughter with open love and affection. Lottie stared back just as fervently, and it was as though the rest of the world ceased to exist for them, save for each other.

In that instant, Lizzy's fears eased. She could see how much he loved Lottie, and how the love was reciprocated. They were so young, but she recognized love when she saw it, and they did as well. Other than mild concern about their age, her objections fell away.

She doubted it would be so easy to win over Mr. Darcy though. He would no doubt consider wealth and standing far more important than true, if young, love. Lizzy had no wish to set herself at odds against her daughter's future father-in-law after they had clashed in the past, but she determined right then and there that she would help their children fight for happiness, even if it meant fighting Mr. Darcy himself.

Chapter Two

FITZWILLIAM RECEIVED a missive from his son via express post, perplexed by his son choosing so hasty a dispatch method. He paid the fee and took the letter, and the express rider waited for a moment. "I do not anticipate needing to send an immediate reply."

"Very good, sir." He nodded to Mr. Darcy and left.

Fitzwilliam took the letter into the study, nodding to a passing maid. "Ask Mrs. Wimbley to bring tea please." It was quite strange to think of Mrs. Wimbley when his first instinct was still to say Mrs. Reynolds, though the dear housekeeper had retired just four months before and lived in a cottage on the grounds. He missed the smooth way she ran the house. There was nothing particularly wrong with Mrs. Wimbley's management, except she wasn't Mrs. Reynolds. Fitzwilliam wasn't a man who liked change.

He opened the letter, expecting it to be full of news from his son's visit to Rosings Park to see Lady Catherine, to whom he had gotten quite close over the years, followed by information of his move to London. His son was settling in early at Darcy House but already looking forward to moving into a student apartment near Cambridge. It was a rite of passage for the Darcy men, and Fitzwilliam understood his excitement. He'd undertaken a similar adventure himself many years ago, and in the unlikely accompaniment of George Wickham. It boggled his mind whenever he thought about the friendship he'd once shared with the blackguard.

He settled in to read, at first a smile on his lips as he prepared himself to read a letter full of cheerful news. He started to scowl in moments. His son was certainly cheerful, but he'd lost all common sense. He could only go on and on about Lottie Williams visiting, and what a divine creature she was. When Fitzwilliam reached the line that he planned to propose, he dropped the letter. "I do not think so," he said almost in a roar.

Mrs. Wimbley appeared in the doorway at that moment, and the teapot rattled as she barely clung to the tray. "Mr. Darcy, do you still want tea?" She sounded timid.

He nodded, though he had lost all thirst in his shock and anger.

She scurried forward and set down the tray. As she started to leave, he said, "Have them ready the carriage. No, have them ready Diablo, for I will need to travel quickly."

"Yes, Mr. Darcy." She gave a nervous half-curtsy and rushed from the room, probably thinking he'd lost his mind.

He wasn't the one who had lost his mind. It was his infatuated son. How dare he think he could marry so lowly? The daughter of William Collins, former rector of Hunsford? Preposterous.

It didn't matter that Collins had inherited Longbourn and became a landed gentleman. Technically, she was his son's peer, but only technically. He knew how far beneath the Bennets were in station and wealth compared to the Darcys, and he imagined that could not have changed under Collins' stewardship. No, he simply would not have it.

He wasn't unsympathetic. He reminded himself of that as he sent for his valet to pack his things. He paused for a moment, staring at his visage in the mirror. He looked quite old today, wearing every one of his forty-four years and then some. That reminded him of younger, more carefree days.

He remembered wanting things that weren't wise. There had been heady and foolish times when he'd been at Cambridge, back before he'd understood what a blackguard his friend really was, and there had been other times, such as his friendship with Mr. Bingley, though Fitzwilliam had been more mature by then. He hadn't seen the man in years, but he well remembered the time he'd spent with him at Netherfield. He remembered his infatuation with a young Miss Bennet.

He deliberately tried to force his thoughts away from Miss Elizabeth. Yet his mind was contrary, summoning an image of her. He could see her laughing, often at his expense when they traded barbs during her brief stay at Netherfield while her sister was ill. Then there was the night of the ball, when he had danced with her and nearly kissed her. Only the reminder that he was practically engaged to his cousin and the disadvantages of a match with a Bennet had held him in check. Later, her mother's vulgarity as she revealed herself, as did the rest of her relations, had made him feel like he'd had a lucky escape. He'd taken advantage of that and ridden from Netherfield as soon as he could, not looking back.

At some point, Elizabeth Bennet, likely driven by pure practicality, had married William Collins. He shuddered at imagining the two of them together, and he quickly pushed the idea from his mind. This situation wasn't about the mistake he'd nearly made.

This was about his son's mistake, and preventing it, before the boy could do something disastrous, like truly fall in love with the Collins girl. He refused to allow history to repeat itself, and it was still early enough to prevent his son from making a grave blunder.

Fitzwilliam could understand how beguiling a Bennet woman could be, but he'd resisted his compulsion. He'd managed to do it himself, and he'd tried for Mr. Bingley, who had succumbed in spite of the inadvisability, but he would succeed when it came to William. He would not allow his son to tie his future to a family so far beneath them.

IT TOOK HIM TWO DAYS to cover the distance between Pemberley and Longbourn. He stopped twice for an inn, spending only a few hours each time in his haste to arrive. He hoped to reach Longbourn before his son could issue the disastrous proposal, but whether or not William asked for Miss Collins, he wouldn't be completing the folly. He still required Fitzwilliam's permission to marry until he was one-and-twenty, and he would never have it.

He was exhausted when he rode up the drive to Longbourn. It took him a moment to realize that things had greatly changed. He supposed he'd been expecting everything to be in a state of genteel poverty, so he was surprised to see most of the buildings looked freshly painted, the area had expanded, and there was a new stable waiting when he stopped with his horse.

The crisply uniformed stable hand rushed out to take his horse and directed him to the front of the house. He could have told the boy he knew the way, but he didn't bother. Instead, he just turned and strode in that direction, grasping his walking stick as his cloak flowed around him.

He almost skidded to a halt at the sight of Elizabeth Bennet—no, Elizabeth Collins, he reminded himself sternly—standing on the doorstep. Seeing her again was like taking a punch during sparring at "Gentleman Jackson's." For a moment, he couldn't help recalling how lovely and feisty she had been all those years ago.

She had her arms crossed, looked not at all welcoming, and was clearly girded for battle. "I was wondering when you would come," she said without any other sort of greeting.

His lips pursed. "As soon as I heard of my son's rash actions, I rode for Longbourn. Has he arrived?"

"Indeed. He is a guest of Charles and Jane, for propriety's sake, but he has been for dinner twice in the four days he has been here, and he has spoken to me about marrying Lottie."

He harrumphed. "That must be quite a coup for you, but I assure you, madam, that it will not come to pass. He still requires my permission to marry."

She inclined her head. "I suppose he does, but he seems earnest about it. I had my doubts, but after seeing them together, I do believe they love each other, Mr. Darcy."

"He is a Darcy and not subject to the luxury of marrying for love."

"Of course not. We would not want our children to be happy, would we?" There was scathing heat in her tone. "Far better to consign them to a loveless, advantageous marriage." Her lips curled in disgust.

"I have no doubt we would be forced to accept an inadequate dowry, and your connections are quite common. Your relations have exposed themselves as fortune hunters and fools. How could you expect me to endorse such a marriage?"

Lizzy's eyes spat fire at him, reminding him of how attractive he used to find her when they sparred. It was one of the reasons he'd often enticed her into verbal exchanges during their time together at Netherfield, but he tried to temper that now. He couldn't afford to

21

be distracted by an ill-advised attraction any more now than he could back then. "I will not allow him to make this mistake."

"Why not? You nearly made the same mistake yourself, did you not, Mr. Darcy?" She said it in an arch tone, but there was a hint of embarrassment in her expression. That reminded him that he had yet to truly study her, besides her angry expression, and as he looked closer at Lizzy, he found her still a pleasing sight indeed.

She was older now, surely almost thirty-nine, and there was gray at her temples. She had fine lines around her eyes and slightly more pronounced lines around her mouth as though she smiled a lot. That was as he remembered her, and to his shock, his old attraction suddenly flamed fully to life again.

"I wasn't imagining that you nearly kissed me, was I, Mr. Darcy?" As she spoke, she moved closer, lowering her voice. "That would not have done, for you were engaged, but you were tempted, were you not?"

There seemed little point in denying the accusation. "That was my folly, but I will not allow my son to make the same mistake."

Her irritation appeared to deepen. "Yet you did not make the mistake, did you? You ran away when you had the chance, which was, of course, the honorable thing to do, since you were betrothed to Miss Anne."

"Ours was a peculiar kind of betrothal, mostly enacted by our mothers more than us. Truthfully, I never fully proposed to Anne. It just seemed to happen." He shifted slightly in his Hessians, well aware the reason he'd allowed it to happen. He'd wanted to escape the temptation of marrying Lizzy Bennet, and it had been eating at him every day to return to her and declare his intentions.

When he had first arrived at Netherfield, rumors from Mr. Collins had preceded him that he was engaged to Miss Anne, and he had allowed that rumor to stand. It seemed to be the only thing keeping him from straying into pure folly and falling in love with Lizzy Bennet.

Now, as he stared down at her, he wondered if he had been a fool back then. Had he squandered an opportunity at happiness for both himself, Lizzy, and even Anne by taking the easy route? His marriage with Anne had lacked passion, for certain, but he had expected nothing less, because she was more like a sister than anything. He'd never had amorous feelings for her, and she certainly hadn't for him either. How could she have when her dearest love had been her lady's maid, who had come with her to Pemberley?

It had taken Fitzwilliam a few weeks to realize the situation, but when he confronted Anne, she had admitted she was in love with her maid and had been for many years. They had reached an agreement that they would maintain their marriage, for it benefited them both, but once there was an heir, that would be the end of any pretense of marriage, save for public appearances. Neither of them had expected her to die in childbirth.

"Mr. Darcy, are you listening to me?" There was a hint of impatience in Lizzy's tone.

He blinked and looked at her. "Of course. "

"Do you agree then?"

He scowled. "Agree to what?"

"Do you agree that the more barriers we put up between them, the more determined they will be to be together? I have asked them to consider a long courtship followed by a long engagement. If they still feel the same way in a couple of years, then they could marry." Her expression softened slightly. "They rejected the idea soundly but promised to consider it. I do believe their love will endure the test of time, but I would like to give them both a chance to further mature first. I support their decision either way though."

His mouth compressed. "My son will not marry your daughter."

She sighed. "I truly agreed with you when I first heard of their plan, and then I renewed my acquaintance with William. I realized he must have gotten all his pleasantness and even-tempered manner from his mother, for he is nothing like his odious father."

"If you find me so odious, why did you nearly kiss me that night at Netherfield?" The words sprang to his lips before he could stifle the impulse to utter the provocative statement.

She scoffed. "You nearly kissed me."

"Are you claiming you would have pulled away then, Lizzy?" It was highly improper to use her first name, but he was beyond caring, so caught up in his anger and stirring passions.

"Of course." She didn't sound as confident as she'd probably intended, which made him smile slightly.

"Really." His tone was laced with skepticism. Before she could move away, he put his arms around her. She had plenty of time to pull away, but she didn't. She stared at him, looking half-mesmerized, as he put his mouth over hers. A moment later, the kiss they had nearly shared eighteen years before came to fruition, and it was enough to make Fitzwilliam see stars and cause his heart to pound in his chest. No previous kiss in his life, few as they had been, had ever been like that.

Somehow, he managed to pull himself together and step back. "I suppose things must have changed, because you made no effort to escape my odious kiss, Mrs. Collins."

She glared at him. "As a married woman, I became used to odious kisses."

As he realized she was comparing him to that oaf, he glared at her. "Since my son is at Netherfield, I shall adjourn there." With those cold words, he turned and strode back toward the stables. The same stable hand ran into the building as soon as he saw him coming, and he returned with Diablo a moment later.

He was a fine, handsome black horse and a descendent of Goliath's, who had been Fitzwilliam's faithful companion for many years before he got too old for riding. His horse's son was equally impressive, with perhaps even more spirit, and it was a small task for the horse to convey him to Netherfield even though Diablo must be tired after their days of hard riding.

As he rode, he fulminated about Elizabeth Collins, and how she could still discombobulate him. She seemed to fully support the idea of the children marrying, and it was unfathomable to him. Even if Fitzwilliam's son was interested in a girl from a proper family, he wouldn't give his consent to marry at this age.

He was inside Netherfield's fine hall a short time later, and he was bracing himself for an uncomfortable reunion. He hadn't seen Bingley since his friend made the foolish decision to return to Netherfield and marry Jane Bennet. Fitzwilliam hadn't approved and had withdrawn his friendship in protest. If that had bothered Bingley, he'd showed no sign of it.

It was surprising then that he had taken in his son, but Fitzwilliam planned to collect William and depart for London posthaste. Perhaps it would have to be tomorrow, to allow his horse and himself a chance to rest, but they would not impose on the Bingley hospitality, likely to be reluctantly given in Fitzwilliam's case, for long.

The butler led him into a sitting room, where he was surprised to be greeted by Jane Bingley moments later. She was much as he remembered, though there were strands of white in her light blonde hair. Her figure was more rounded, and he assumed she must have birthed a brood for Bingley.

She seemed as gracious as ever, and if she had any idea that he had disapproved of her marriage to Charles and had tried to block it, she gave no indication as she offered a polite greeting and said, "Charles is fishing, but William will be down shortly. I informed him that you are waiting." She gestured for him to take a seat. "May I offer you tea?"

"I am not thirsty." He sat down stiffly as she rang for tea. He started to protest but realized perhaps she wanted some. He doubted she truly wanted to have tea with him though. "You seem quite at home here, Miss Bennet." He inclined his head to her stiffly, his spine straight.

She seemed amused. "Many people call me Mrs. Bingley these days, Mr. Darcy." She sounded calm as she made the gentle rebuke. "Did you have a pleasant trip?"

"No. I rode hard to prevent this foolishness. I have come to recover my son. We shall leave as soon as we can arrange travel."

Jane murmured something that could have been considered noncommittal as a housemaid appeared, and she asked for a tray of tea. She seemed disapproving of him, and the idea rankled. Yet her words were a contrast to what he'd expected when next she spoke. "Young Mr. Darcy is a fine young man. You must be quite proud of him."

"Indeed," he said distantly. "He is a fine man with fine breeding and great prospects."

"Those prospects do not include my niece," said Jane in a neutral tone. Obviously, she had grown wiser to subtleties and slights over the years.

He nodded. "Precisely."

"I do believe you might reevaluate that when you see them together, Mr. Darcy." She didn't speak to him again as they waited for tea. She seemed perfectly content in the silence, but he was distracted from having to dwell on it when William appeared in the doorway. He was gratified to see his son looked slightly nervous.

As William walked toward him, his shoulders straight and spine stiff, he seemed resolved. He resembled Fitzwilliam in many ways, though he had some of Anne's features too. It was a harmonious blend that made him attractive, and he would have no trouble obtaining a far more suitable wife with his wealth and social position. He could even have a titled heiress if he set his mind to it.

"I do beg your pardon, Mrs. Bingley, but might I speak with my father alone? I do not wish to be rude, but I do not believe this will be a happy meeting."

Fitzwilliam was surprised at his son's poise as he made the unusual request of the hostess of the house. He held his tongue, tempted to rebuke his son for his display of ill manners, but it was better for Jane Bingley to depart.

She excused herself a moment later with a nod to both of them. If she was bothered by the request, she didn't give any indication.

"You have received my letter," said William in a resigned tone as he sat on the settee Mrs. Bingley had previously occupied.

"I have, and you will not marry so young, and not to one of her breeding. She is Elizabeth Collins' daughter."

He frowned. "That is a strange objection upon which to focus, Papa. Is it because she is Mrs. Collins' daughter, or because she is Mr. Collins' daughter? On what grounds do you object?"

"I object on the grounds the girl has no dowry, no social standing, and she is impossibly unworthy to be your wife. Her family would humiliate you and our name." As he said the words, he remembered telling himself the same things over and over again many years before when he was standing in this very library, having just exchanged words with Miss Bennet that had made him want to smile and follow behind her to ask to continue the conversation.

He blinked, forcing the memory from his mind so he could focus on the present. "There are far more suitable candidates to be a Darcy bride."

"Perhaps, but none of them speak to my heart the way Lottie does."

Fitzwilliam huffed a sigh of impatience. "It is a brief infatuation, and you have known each other for six weeks. It is preposterous that you could be in love upon such short acquaintance." As he said that, he felt a slight niggle of discomfort at uttering the words, realizing they weren't entirely true. It had taken him about the same amount of time to fall...to become infatuated with Miss Bennet. Still, that had definitely not proven strong enough for marriage, and it had to be the same for Miss Collins and William.

"Papa, I have known Lottie for many years, and our love has grown from friendship to something more. I am resolved in this matter and will marry her."

"If you try to go through with this, I will completely disown you. I shall not give my permission to marry her. You will have to wait until you are twenty-one and will be penniless."

"I am prepared to do so if I must. Fortunately, if you choose to disown me, that is acceptable. I have already been given permission by Mrs. Collins to stay with them if the need arises. She warned me that you were likely to disinherit me for this choice."

Fitzwilliam scowled at how calmly his son was accepting the threat, and also that Lizzy had perceived he would issue it. The last thing he wanted to do was disown his son. "I am simply asking you to see reason, my boy. You must see you are too young, and she is not the right woman for you."

"I understand your misgivings, Papa, but I cannot ignore what my heart tells me. I am not like you. It is not in my nature to put practicality above happiness. Obviously, I do not remember my mother, but I suspect she might have been the same."

"Anne certainly believed in following her heart, but she understood the need for practicality." Some of the fire went out of him as he thought about his wife. He and Anne had been good friends, and he was certain she would have been a good mother. He couldn't help thinking she would have supported their son, and she probably would have approved of Lizzy's idea of asking the children to undertake a long courtship to decide if that was what they truly wanted. Still, he wasn't going to concede without protest. "You know the terms then."

"I do." William bowed to him. "I take my leave."

Fitzwilliam watched William depart before he followed a short time later. He was surprised to see no one waiting for him in the hall, including Mrs. Bingley or Bingley. A maid appeared a few moments later and directed him to a room for his use, and he remembered his valet wasn't with him. That had proved to be quite inconvenient, but he'd ridden hard, and bringing along Baston would only have slowed his progress. Perhaps he could borrow a servant for the night.

He moved across the room, intent on issuing the request, and as he glanced out the window, he caught sight of his son walking below him. There was a lovely girl beside him, and she was not exactly a replica of Lizzy Bennet from nearly twenty years ago, but she was close enough that he had no trouble recognizing her as Lottie Collins.

The way they stood together, his hands enfolding hers before he lifted them to his mouth to give a kiss to the back of hers, spoke of such tenderness between them that he was moved by the sight. Feeling uncomfortable with eavesdropping, but wanting to know of what they were speaking, he opened his window, hoping to catch a snippet of their conversation.

"It was as Mrs. Collins warned me," said William.

Lottie gasped. "Your papa has disowned you?"

Fitzwilliam's lips tightened as he resisted the urge to defend himself. No doubt, her ardor would cool now that she knew William would be penniless.

"He has issued the threat." William sounded remarkedly unconcerned. "It has no bearing on how I feel. Nothing has changed."

He held his breath as Lottie shook her head, fully expecting her to now reject his son.

"Oh, William, I do not want to cause strife between you and your father. I know how you love and admire Mr. Darcy, and he has set the standard for the man you are."

He frowned at the words, finding them unexpected and disconcerting.

His son stiffened his spine. "I do admire my father, but in this, he is wrong. I would give up everything for you, Lottie."

The girl hesitated for a moment, and he was sure she'd find a way out of the proposal now. Instead, she said, "I should not encourage you to be so noble. I suppose I should tell you to forget about our love and live the life that would best please your father to secure your position and relationship with him, but I am too selfish for that. I love you so much, William, to the detriment of my honor and your future."

His eyes widened at the words.

"It is no sacrifice to give up Pemberley and the Darcy fortune. I shall only regret my father turning from me, for he will be sad and lonely. I will miss him, but my heart belongs to you, and I am resolved."

A moment later, William kissed Lottie with far more passion than was permissible, but Fitzwilliam could hardly protest lest he reveal he was listening to them.

Lottie seemed on the verge of tears, but she sounded reasonably composed when the kiss ended, and she spoke again. "I love you, William. I would marry you if both our parents disowned us and cast us into wretched deprivation."

He couldn't resist rolling his eyes at that, though the young lady seemed sincere.

"I would do the same. If there is too much objection, we will run to Gretna Green."

Lottie frowned. "I would hope to avoid such a dishonorable course, but if it is the only way to be together…"

"It seems unlikely to come to that with your mother's support, dearest. I pray my father will someday understand the depths of my emotions, but if not, I can live without his approval. I could never live without you."

The two entwined again.

As he eased away from the window and closed it quietly, Fitzwilliam realized he had been wrong. He hadn't even considered William and Lottie's perspectives and feelings. He had been so hell-bent on stopping the union because of the Collins connections and the taint of the past linking him to Lizzy Bennet that he hadn't really given it a thought that his son might truly love Lottie Collins.

After having observed them, he was left questioning everything he'd believed. Was social standing and wealth that much more important than his son's happiness? Was he automatically rejecting Miss Collins based on her family and his own nebulous feelings for Lizzy? He leaned against the wall and closed his eyes as the weight of guilt threatened to crush him. He was being a judgmental fool, and his preconceptions would consign his son to a life of unhappiness if he had his way.

Fitzwilliam well knew how a loveless marriage could drain one's enthusiasm for life. He and Anne had a true accord and close relationship, but there had always been her lover between them, and truthfully, his own feelings for Miss Bennet had intruded as well. He still bore lingering qualms about the path he'd taken. He didn't want William to look back and feel the same regret in years to come.

Chapter Three

HER DAUGHTER AND INTENDED had just departed after sharing the news that his father had forbade the match, planning to walk to Oakham Mount in the accompaniment of Mary, who offered to act as chaperone. They were both dejected, but Lizzy had striven to be supportive and hide her ire while speaking to them.

Lizzy hadn't been surprised, but she had been disappointed that Fitzwilliam Darcy had resorted to such means. She hadn't truly known whether he would make such an ultimatum when she'd warned William two days ago, but she remembered how he had ceased all friendship with Charles after hearing about his friend's intention to marry Jane. Yet, a friendship could never be as close as a father/son relationship, so she'd hoped he wouldn't sink so low.

She was angry and not fit company when the aging Hill shuffled in to announce a visitor. She thought it might be Jane, come to commiserate with the young lovers, and she certainly wasn't expecting it to be Fitzwilliam Darcy standing in the doorway when she left the sitting room.

Lizzy got over her shock after a moment and said, "Good afternoon, Mr. Darcy." She was struggling to be civil and pretend like the earlier exchange hadn't happened, and that she wasn't furious that he was hurting both their children due to his pride. Never mind her lips were still buzzing from the feel of his kiss against them. She should be shocked and outraged at his maneuver, rather than remembering how it had made her feel even into her toes, which had tingled and curled as their lips shared a tender moment.

"I wish to speak to you, Mrs. Collins." He sounded far humbler this time, which was certainly a surprise.

"Of course." Feeling slightly confused, since he was confounding her expectations, she led him down the hallway and into her study. It had once been her father's library, and it still functioned for that purpose too, but Lizzy also conducted most of the estate business from there. She gestured for him to take a seat across from her as she sat in the familiar chair that had once been her father's. "I truly did not expect you back so soon." She winced slightly at blurting out her thoughts. "Pardon my manners. May I offer you tea?"

He looked around the study for moment, eyes wide, as he shook his head. "No, thank you. I am fine. I do not believe I ever saw this room when it was Mr. Bennet's, but it appears you have not changed much."

She frowned. "What gives you that idea?"

He gestured to the entire wall of books on estate management. "Surely, those must have been your father's?"

"Some, though I have acquired many over the years since. My father was not quite as adept at estate management and saving as he could have been."

"Was Mr. Collins an adept manager?"

She considered not answering, for she never liked to discuss that time in her life, but she had nothing to hide. She just preferred not to dwell on her short marriage to Mr. Collins. "Mr. Collins appeared to be of the same bent, along with the flaw of stinginess, while assuming he knew more than everyone around him. When the plow was stuck in the ground, he insisted he would be able to get it out when no one else could, not wanting to pay for extra assistance. That proved to be his downfall, quite literally." She flushed as she said that. "I do not mean to be flippant, of course. The poor man stumbled and fell on one of the tines, and it ran him through."

"I take it you were not married very long then?"

Lizzy shook her head. "It was a very brief marriage, and two good things came from it—Lottie, and being able to control Longbourn."

He raised a brow. "Surely, you have a male guardian who oversees business for you, or perhaps a steward?"

She clenched her teeth, unsurprised he underestimated her. Most men did. "Of course, I have a steward, but I do not need a man to manage my property. Mr. Bingley was quite helpful in the beginning, as was my steward. I suppose, ostensibly, there is a male figurehead in the picture. Mr. Bingley occasionally has to sign things for me, which is quite irritating, but all of Longbourn's success is owed to me."

She spoke without false modesty, aware of the accomplishments she had achieved over the last several years. Particularly with being hindered by the patriarchal constraints of society, she had managed a great deal.

He seemed somewhere between impressed and unsettled. "You have done well with Longbourn then?"

Rather than answer directly, she said, "You expressed concerns about my daughter's dowry."

"It is not truly that important, except it matters in my social circle. My son does not need to marry for wealth as my poor cousin Richard did."

She smiled for a moment. "I have met the colonel a few times. He seems quite content with his lovely wife."

Fitzwilliam nodded. "I believe he truly loves Violet, but it did not hurt that her father was a wealthy merchant. Fortunately,

William does not need to consider such things to make a suitable match."

She inclined her head. "I understand. Lottie is in a similar position."

His eyes narrowed, and he sounded skeptical. "Indeed?"

"I learned from my father's poor example, though I suppose I was fortunate to only have to provide for one daughter. I have set aside ten thousand pounds for Lottie's dowry."

Fitzwilliam looked like he nearly choked, and she was glad he hadn't accepted her offer of tea, or he likely would have sprayed it all over both of them. He cleared his throat, appearing shocked beyond reason. "Ten thousand pounds?"

She took great pleasure and a strong dash of pride in nodding tightly. "With a further one thousand pounds per year for maintenance."

He sputtered. "How can you possibly afford that? You do not need to put yourself in deep debt. If I decide to approve the match, dowry would not matter."

"It does though. It assures my daughter has funds of her own and a way to take care of herself. I will not have her in a situation where she is forced to marry someone she does not love to take care of herself or others. That has been a driving motivation for me as I built up Longbourn to what it used to be before my father mismanaged it." She shuddered at the slightly disloyal words, but they were true.

"He was a good father in some ways, but mostly, he was self-absorbed. I have not made the same mistakes. My daughter is well provided for, and though she doesn't have the same social standing as your son, I had planned to send her to London for a Season after Christmastide. She will find a good husband there—or she would have, but she appears to already be settled on your son."

"You did not have a Season." He uttered it as an observation and still seemed to be trying to absorb her claims. He had no reason to doubt them, and she'd soundly assure him of that if he indicated disbelief.

"I did not. Neither did my sisters, for my parents considered it unfair to fund a Season for only one. Lottie asked for a Season last year, but I expect her to marry in her first Season, as beautiful, kind, and accomplished as she is in drawing, dancing, and modern languages, so I selfishly told her to wait another year. I cannot regret that, for she seems to be happy with William, and whether they choose a short or long betrothal, I support their union."

"My son mentioned as much." He scowled at her. "He indicated you have offered him refuge here if I disown him."

"I did, for he seems like a sensible and sweet young man. He must get that from his mother." She almost laughed at the way his lips pursed. "I must admit, I had my reservations when she first told me he was coming to propose, but all it took was observing them quietly for a few minutes alone to realize there is genuine love and affection between them, Mr. Darcy."

"Perhaps, but is it enduring?"

She was surprised at his small concession. "I do not know if it is enough to last them a lifetime, and if perhaps they might outgrow their sentiments, so I still stand by my urging of a longer courtship and engagement, but I will not insist upon it. If you choose to disown the boy, he will find a home here with us. After all, I need someone trained in how to run Longbourn when I have passed. I had planned to teach Lottie, but it would be sensible for them both to know."

He seemed uncomfortable as he shifted. "I saw them together too." He spoke abruptly, clearly unhappy with those words and the admission he had to make. "They appear to have a strong bond between them. I could see the affection between them. They are willing to sacrifice for each other, and though I am not entirely convinced due to their tender age, I will withdraw my objections."

She blinked, shocked to hear that. "Truly?"

He frowned at her. "I am capable of revising my opinions upon occasion."

She snorted. "If I recall from many years ago, you are not one to change your opinion once it is set, according to Caroline." Her lips twitched as she recalled that time, back when Caroline had been so very haughty and convinced she could set her cap for Mr. Darcy despite his engagement. Of course, she must have known, unlike the locals of Meryton, that it hadn't been formally announced yet and still had hope.

Fortunately, Caroline had mellowed over the years and was content with Mr. Carter, the man she had married the year following the Darcy/de Bourgh union. She was also far more pleasant these days, to Lizzy's relief, since they saw each other at least a few times per year, with her sister married to Caroline's brother.

"I do not write my opinions in stone," he said in a harsh manner.

"I have seen very little evidence of that, Mr. Darcy. For example, when Mr. Bingley returned to court my sister again and proposed, you cut off all contact with him. You have maintained your stubborn silence for eighteen years, have you not? I merely question whether you can truly change your mind so quickly."

He shifted in his seat. "I would like my son to be happy." He seemed to speak from the heart when he said that. He cleared his throat and looked down. "Truthfully, Anne and I did not have the happiest of marriages. We were good friends, but I loved her like a sister, not a wife. It is very difficult to have a good marriage with someone you consider a sister, especially when she loves another."

Lizzy nodded slowly, startled to hear Anne had maintained a *tendre* for another. "In my case, it was very difficult to have a good marriage with someone I could not respect. I tried to make the union work, and he seemed to genuinely try too, but Mr. Collins was never a good match for me. If my father had not died the very day you left Netherfield, I never would have accepted his proposal."

Fitzwilliam winced. "I am sorry. I had not heard that detail."

"I am surprised Lady Catherine didn't say anything to you about it."

"My aunt and I are not particularly close."

Lizzy couldn't hide her disapproval. "Which is unfortunate, because once you get past her overbearing manner, you can find a genuinely lovely woman inside. She wants what is best for you and for everyone. The only problem arises if you deviate from the course she has deemed best for you." Her lips twitched as she added that.

He seemed surprised. "You sound fond of my aunt."

"Surprisingly, I am. She proved to be an unexpected ally once we got past our differences when I was at Hunsford. I think she liked that I stood up to her. She has gotten quite close to my family over the years, and I know she shall want to be included in Lottie's engagement party."

He frowned. "What happened to a long courtship?"

Lizzy shrugged. "I am being realistic. I do not believe they have it in them to wait long. For that matter, perhaps it is best to let them marry sooner rather than later, for young love is quite intense, and passions can run high. There could be...indelicate complications if we try to make them wait too long."

He surprised her by standing up and moving around the desk. Lizzy refused to yield any ground, but she trembled a little inside as he leaned closer, propping himself against the corner of her desk. "It is not always young passions that run strong, is it?" As he asked, he trailed his knuckle down her cheek and pushed a stray hair that escaped her chignon behind her ear.

Lizzy's mouth went dry at the casual touch, and she couldn't help recalling the way he'd kissed her earlier. It had been tinged with anger, but this time, she wanted a different memory.

It had been a long time since she'd acted impulsively, forced as she had been to be disciplined and think of everyone's future and all that was at stake with a wrong choice, but as he leaned down, she stretched up, and their lips met.

This was a far different kiss than the angry one they had exchanged earlier in the afternoon. It was gentle, but there was certainly a surging inferno of passion underlying it. She put her arms around his neck as she stood up the rest of the way, and he pulled her against him.

Lizzy had kissed a man before, and of course, she had lain with one, but Mr. Collins had never managed to make her senses feel like this, like every nerve in her body was strung taut in a blazing conflagration. When Fitzwilliam moved his mouth, nibbling on her ear before sucking on her neck, she whimpered and pushed herself closer to him.

Only catching sight of them in the mirror across the way brought her back to her senses, and she gently pushed him from her. "This is hardly the time or place for that sort of thing." How prim and proper she sounded, though she didn't feel that way at all.

He cleared his throat and straightened his shoulders. "Quite right. I must speak with my son anyway. I suppose there will be contracts to negotiate and a betrothal party to plan."

She nodded her agreement, remaining where she stood as he walked around her desk and headed for the door. When he paused in the doorway to look back, she held her breath as he said, "This is not over between us, Lizzy. I walked away long ago, and though I suppose it worked out for the best, because we couldn't have the lives we have now, I cannot help feeling an ache of remorse. I would like to know what might have been and what could still be."

She was incapable of answering him, shocked as she was by the revelation, though it shouldn't have been all that surprising in light of the fact they had kissed each other twice in since their reunion. She was still afraid though. What would he want from her? She was a widow, which put her in a position to enjoy certain delights of the flesh that a young maiden hadn't been deemed entitled to indulge. Did he want something from her that was strictly physical, or was he thinking of something more?

Lizzy watched him go, still not certain how to feel.

Chapter Four

TIME SEEMED TO SPEED past, and two fortnights had gone in the blink of an eye. It had been a busy month with the contract negotiations and announcing the engagement, followed by the party planned for that evening. Lady de Bourgh had arrived the day before, and Lizzy was concerned by how frail she seemed. When she entered the sitting room and found Lady Catherine showing Lottie an intricate dance step from a dance no longer in fashion, she asked, "What are you doing, Lady Catherine? You should be resting."

"I am not so old that I cannot manage a small dance step, particularly on the eve of the ball." Lady Catherine sounded annoyed by her fussing, but Lizzy suspected she secretly liked it. She'd always liked someone to defer to her, though contrarily, it seemed that was the reason she liked Lizzy—her refusal to do so.

She didn't want to treat her any differently than she had, but she was still concerned for her. "Have you seen the apothecary recently?"

Lady Catherine huffed at her as she sat down, accepting a cup of tea from Lottie, who was glowing with excitement. "Of course not. Only sick people see the apothecary. I am not sick, dear girl. I am merely getting old. It happens to everyone, if they are fortunate enough to live to a ripe age." She frowned, seeming to be thinking of her daughter, and Lizzy patted her hand in a show of sympathy as she pretended it was just to offer her the bowl of sugar.

After Lady Catherine had added a couple of lumps, Lizzy said, "I do not mean to fuss. I worry about you."

"I do appreciate it, dear girl, but it is unnecessary. I feel fine and in good health. I shall enjoy life until I am no longer able to do so. Tonight, we shall celebrate this engagement of my grandson to my goddaughter, and we shall all be quite jug-bitten fools by morning."

Lizzy smiled, hardly able to imagine Catherine being intoxicated, though it was amusing.

Shortly thereafter, they all went separate ways to prepare for the ball, and Lizzy stopped at her mother's room to check on Fanny, who was having what sounded like a nervous episode. She peeked in through the doorway, discovering Fanny was simply looking for her pearls and asking the maid where they might have gotten to as she bemoaned her nerves being overwrought with all the excitement.

Lizzy smiled, not interceding, as she made her way to her bedroom. Her maid was waiting, and she was dressed within a couple of hours. She couldn't help feeling a faint stirring of excitement for the forthcoming ball at Netherfield. It had so many echoes of the past, though she hoped this evening ended differently for everyone than the last one had.

Chapter Five

FITZWILLIAM WAS BROODING in the corner, nursing a cup of smoking bishop, when Lady de Bourgh approached him. He nodded to his aunt respectfully as he lowered the cup of punch he'd been about to sip. "Good evening, Lady Catherine."

She smiled. "You are always so formal, Fitzwilliam."

"I am a product of my upbringing."

"Yes, shamefully so sometimes."

He scowled. "I beg your pardon?"

"My sister and her husband raised you to be a good master, but you were also raised to think less of those beneath you. It is a failing of all in our social circle, my boy. I did the same thing with Anne, though she was naturally a kind girl, and she always treated the servants well."

Fitzwilliam's lips twitched as he recalled the moment he had realized just how close Anne was to her maid. He'd walked in on them kissing, and her secret had been revealed. He nodded his agreement. "She was very kind, particularly to her maid."

Catherine looked uncomfortable for a moment. "I suspected." She practically whispered that.

He arched brow. "What?"

"I suspected she and the girl were quite good *friends*." She flushed as she said it. "I had hoped her *preferences* would change with marriage."

He blinked in shock. "Yes, they were quite good *friends*, and that never changed." Clearing his throat, he said, "It was difficult to be married to someone who would absolutely never fall in love with me. Truthfully, I could never have loved Anne the way I should have either though."

He expected his revelation to anger his aunt, so it surprised him when she just nodded. "I have realized that as the years passed, and I have had time to think. I forced you two into fueling the dream your mother and I had, but it was never what either of you wanted. I suspect you would not have yielded if something had not pushed you into accepting the course." She arched a brow expectantly.

"It is true that I do not do what I do not wish to do. I am a Darcy."

"You are a proud Darcy. There is nothing wrong with being prideful, for you have a great many accomplishments of which to be proud, as long as you temper that with humility and compassion. Do not let pride and your own insistence on maintaining certain social standards prevent you from having happiness a second time, Fitzwilliam."

He frowned at her. "I do not know what you mean, madam."

Lady Catherine gave him a knowing look as she glanced across the room, where Lizzy stood with her daughter and his son. "Do you not, my boy? I do not know all the details, but I pieced together enough over the years to realize there was at least some level of affection between you and Lizzy. If you had been flexible enough to act upon it then, our lives would have been quite different. I must confess, in some ways I would have been happy for that, because if Anne had not borne William, she would still be alive. Yet I cannot stand to think that way either, because I am quite fond of my grandson." She squeezed his hand. "I am fond of my nephew as well, and I only want your contentment. I do believe you could be happy with Lizzy."

Fitzwilliam blinked. "Are you encouraging me to pursue her?"

"Indeed I am. I suppose if circumstances had conspired to bring you back together sooner, I would have tried to play matchmaker then, but I saw the affection between Lottie and William forming over the years, and I assumed time would settle old wounds and bring happiness for everyone, so I abided."

He shook his head. "You are truly trying to claim victory for bringing the children together and inadvertently bringing Lizzy back into my life?"

"Certainly. After all, I am a Matlock, and we are a proud bunch as well." She spoke heartily, but she winked at him. "I do believe you should go claim a dance before a certain lady's card is full."

Fitzwilliam cleared his throat and handed her his punch, which she took with a small smile. Her encouragement got him across the room, but his courage nearly deserted him when he stood before her. He realized after a moment she was staring at him awkwardly, and he hadn't returned her greeting. "Dance with me." That was hardly what he'd planned to say, and it certainly wasn't eloquent, but he didn't even wait for her acceptance. He just took her hand and led her onto the floor.

"What if I have this dance reserved for another?" She sounded politely curious as she stepped into formation.

"They must be quite aggrieved at missing out on the opportunity to dance with you." He spoke firmly, not intending to yield.

"Fortunately for you, this dance has not yet been claimed."

"Perhaps you were saving it for me?"

"Such cheek to suggest that. Your ego must be enormous, Mr. Darcy."

"Among many things," he said with a suggestive laugh.

Her eyes widened, and she blushed lightly, but she obviously wasn't too shocked. It was refreshing to be able to speak with her a little more candidly than he had when she was younger and still a maiden.

"You seemed to have a deep conversation with Lady Catherine."

"My aunt was giving me sage advice. She suggested I had waited too long and was too proud of my own name to yield and allow some happiness in my life."

"Perhaps she is correct." Lizzy lowered her voice slightly. "What sort of happiness do you seek, Fitzwilliam?"

"I would like to lose myself in your arms, Lizzy." He growled the words softly, knowing he was standing too close to her but unable to care.

Fortunately, she maintained some sense of decorum because she stepped back. "In that case, when the dance ends, I plan to leave the room. I will be in the library, and perhaps you will find me there."

He could barely hold back the anticipation as he nodded, and when the song ended, he bowed to her as he was supposed to, but it was painful to watch her walk away. He observed her exit the room, and he spent a few moments in conversation with Bingley, who was far more courteous than Fitzwilliam deserved. He had been gracious since the day Fitzwilliam approached him to apologize weeks ago, and they were slowly regaining vestiges of their old friendship. Fitzwilliam was surprised by how much he had missed having Bingley in his life, and he realized that was yet another thing his pride had cost him.

When he felt like enough time had elapsed, he slipped away from the ballroom. He went down the hall, well familiar with the path to the Netherfield library, and entered it. The door was open, but he took a moment to close and lock it as he caught sight of Lizzy standing by the fireplace. He moved over to stand behind her, putting his arms around her. It felt good to hold her.

Chapter Six

LIZZY MOANED WHEN HIS arms wrapped around her, making no effort to free herself. She recognized his scent, but it was unlikely to be anyone else anyway. Passion coursed through her, stirring desires long forgotten and never realized.

"My Lizzy," he whispered against her ear as his lips nibbled on her lobe.

She shivered in response. "Fitzwilliam." She arched her neck to allow him better access, and he accepted the invitation by sucking at the bend of her neck and shoulder. Warmth coursed through her, and she trembled at his touch.

He cupped one of her breasts in his palm, and it was a snug fit, since her figure had changed after giving birth and over the passing years. She moaned again as he lightly tugged her nipple while nibbling on her neck.

She was suddenly desperate to feel his arms around her properly, so she pulled away to turn and face him. Lizzy cupped his face in her hands and stretched upward to brush her lips against his. Her kiss was almost tentative, but he pulled her closer, deepening it into a much more passionate exchange.

Fitzwilliam's tongue surged inside her mouth, and her eyes widened. She'd never been kissed this way before. Indeed, she hadn't really considered it would be possible. Her few kisses with Mr.

Collins had been perfunctory, just like their coupling, which had never moved her. She had merely endured it.

She was embracing this exchange with enthusiasm, and she stroked her tongue against his after a second of shyness. He trembled and groaned, and she did it again. Her hands wandered along his body, stymied by his waistcoat and cravat. She desperately wanted to feel the flesh beneath, but she wasn't confident she could help return him to his previous state of order after they indulged their passions.

That almost cooled her ardor. The harsh reminder that this was just a delayed culmination of the passions they'd felt years ago threatened to rip her from the fantasy. She desperately rejected the notion, clinging to the moment instead of worrying about the future. It lent a new air of desperation to her as she stroked his chest and slipped a hand under the fall of his pants.

"Lizzy." There was a hint of a growl in his voice, and he trembled as she stroked the length of him. Was he warning her or encouraging her?

She was too enamored with exploration to heed any warning. She felt the length of him, surprised by his solid warmth and girth. It had been a long time since she'd lain with a man, and Fitzwilliam felt a little intimidating. She squeezed her hand around his shaft without thought.

"Lizzy," he said again in that same growly tone as he picked her up and laid her on the settee. "You threaten all my control."

She smiled, though she still had a hint of anxiety. "I am pleased to hear that."

He laughed, though it seemed strained, as he laid atop her. His mouth covered hers again, and she lost herself in his kisses as his hands delved into her bodice, carefully easing it down and fussing with her corset and chemise to free her breasts.

She shivered at the cool air against them, but she didn't push him away. She wanted this. She needed and deserved tonight. Tomorrow's regrets, if any, could wait until then. When he slid down her body to take her nipple in his mouth, she gasped at the pleasure. She'd never experienced such a thing before.

"So lovely." He whispered the praise as he lifted his head. "Your skin is so soft, and your body is so welcoming."

Her eyes widened as he shifted, pushing up her skirt on one leg and settling between her thighs. It felt as though they'd been made to fit together. When he started stroking her quim, she trembled. "What are you...?" She trailed off with a gasp as he pressed more firmly against a particularly sensitive area. It felt hard yet soft, and she was aware it could be pleasurable to touch, but she'd never explored the area. It struck her as absurd to have avoided touching places on her own body for almost thirty-nine years, especially if it could evoke such sensations.

The touch of his fingers paled in comparison when he shifted them again, lifting her higher up the settee and resettling himself so his mouth covered her mound instead. Lizzy clenched her hands in his hair and tried to stifle the urge to scream as his mouth explored her. She shifted and writhed, never knowing such a feeling was possible. Just when she was convinced it couldn't get better, a new sensation overtook her.

Giddiness swept over her, leaving her head spinning and her heart racing. She clutched him tightly against her as she spasmed and convulsed, her sheath tightening in its need to be filled as she bucked against him. A crescendo of pleasure overtook her, and there were stars behind her eyes, even though she'd closed them in the throes of her bliss.

"You look beautiful that way, love," said Fitzwilliam with a masculine chuckle. He seemed pleased with himself as he reoriented them once more.

He had reason to be. She could concede that, even as she was perturbed she'd gone so long without this kind of pleasure in her ignorance of the possibilities. She managed to open her hazy eyes to focus on him as his shaft pressed against her quim. Taking a deep breath to steel herself, she recalled how painful this part always was.

To her shock, he slid into her with only a little resistance and mild discomfort. She was slick and waiting for him, and she'd never been prepared before. No wonder it had hurt. With Fitzwilliam, any discomfort soon faded to pleasure as he thrust into her. She could see he was on the edge of obtaining his own release, and she was so focused on ensuring his pleasure that she didn't realize she was on the cusp again as well until another climax rocked her.

Fitzwilliam spilled into her a moment later, and then he held her tightly against him as they remained locked together. His forehead was against hers, and their mingled harsh breathing filled the room for several moments until the exertion of passion passed.

"I am glad you found me in the library, Fitzwilliam." Lizzy shivered slightly as she laid under him. "I felt like I had been waiting for this all night."

"More like eighteen years." His lips pressed against her neck for a minute before he whispered, "I was a fool to wait so long."

"Perhaps, but our lives have unfolded the way they should have, and maybe we are finally ready to deal with our feelings for each other." As much as she regretted the time she'd lost with Fitzwilliam, she could never regret having Lottie. She also still had no idea exactly what he wanted from her anyway.

"I am more than ready. There is something I must ask you." As he said that, he turned them on their sides, facing each other. "I love you, Lizzy."

Her eyes widened at the declaration. Even in the midst of their shared passions, she hadn't been certain his feelings ran that deeply. "You do?"

"I do. It took me far too long to admit it, but it is true. How do you feel about me?"

"I find you dashing and far too easy to love as well, Fitzwilliam. That is why I am willing to embark on an affair with you." She held her breath as she said that, her heart crying out for more even as she tried to seem like a practical, experienced widow despite feeling like a virgin who'd newly discovered the power of desire.

He looked stunned. "You believe all I want is an affair?"

She nibbled on her lower lip. "I do not know what to think. I am certainly below you in social standing and wealth, and all the objections you once had still stand. My family is less of a trial now, but Fanny will be my albatross for the rest of her life, which I hope is long and happy. Since I am a widowed woman, I assumed you only wanted a physical dalliance."

He looked injured before his expression morphed to anger. "You assumed wrongly. I will marry you or nothing."

She blinked, and happiness slowly expanded in her chest, making her feel giddy. "Was that a proposal?"

He nodded. "Indeed, it was. You will marry me, or you will not have me at all."

"When you put it in such a persuasive way, how can I refuse?" To soften the words, she leaned forward and kissed him on the cheek. "If that is what you truly desire, I will marry you. I did not have the best experience with the institution the first time around, but I am confident I will be happier with you than I ever could have been with Mr. Collins."

"I shall tell you all about my loveless marriage with Anne someday as well, but suffice to say, there was no room in her heart for anyone else because she loved another—and truthfully, so did I. It was an unsatisfactory marriage for both of us, save for William. Even then, poor Anne had to sacrifice everything."

"That must have been awful for both of you."

"I confess, I greeted being a widower with a hint of relief. It was not because I did not like Anne or want to spend time with her, but I did not love her. There was freedom from that burden with her passing, though it was a shameful way to feel."

Lizzy nodded. "Perhaps, but I understand. I was more than relieved. When Mr. Collins died, I was almost giddy, which shamed me, but it was like being released from a life sentence. It makes me sound like a horrible person to say it that way, but it was how I felt. I was sad at his death, but I was happy my life with him was over."

"That is precisely how it was. We were not with people who would make us happy, but we have a chance to rectify that. And now I ask you properly—will you marry me, Lizzy?"

"I would be thrilled to marry you, Fitzwilliam." When he pulled her tighter into his arms, she kissed him with all the passion that had burned between them, banked but never completely smothered, and it was a long time before they managed to pull away from each other and return to the ball. It was so late they nearly missed the formal betrothal announcement.

After Lizzy had shared a toast with the attendees, she caught sight of Lady Catherine standing in the corner. The older woman wore a satisfied smirk and inclined her head in Lizzy's direction with a knowing gleam in her gaze. If she realized what Lizzy and Fitzwilliam had slipped away to do, she clearly approved.

Epilogue

IT WAS PERHAPS SLIGHTLY unconventional, but since they already had a wedding planned, it seemed easy enough to add a second couple, so three weeks later, Lizzy stood beside her soon-to-be husband and her daughter, who stood next to William. The vicar conducted the double ceremony, and Lizzy was teary-eyed, uncertain if she was crying because her daughter looked so beautiful or because she was finally getting a chance at her own happiness. Perhaps it was a combination of both emotions that left her gaze blurry with moisture.

When Fitzwilliam kissed her as the vicar announced the couples as husband and wife and husband and wife, she wanted to cling to him. Instead, she forced a hint of decorum and stepped back before turning to face the congregation. Only a few of their friends and family attended, with most planning to come for the wedding breakfast, but Lady Catherine was at the front row, standing beside Fanny and beaming as though she had been the architect of it all.

Lizzy was certain as the story gained momentum and changed with retelling, that by the time another eighteen years had passed, Lady Catherine would be claiming the credit for bringing them all together. Lizzy didn't mind. She didn't care who received acclaim as long as she got to reap the rewards. After a lifetime of waiting, it was finally her turn to be happy, and she was certain she would find only happiness with Fitzwilliam as the years passed, and their lives entwined more and more.

There would be grandchildren from Lottie and William, and perhaps even more children for her and Fitzwilliam. There would be highs and lows, and she knew they would still argue upon occasion, since that was their nature, but a strong foundation of love would support them through anything. It had lasted with barely any nurturing for almost two decades, and it was sure to grow and further strengthen now with proper tending.

"Are you happy, Mama?" asked Lottie as they left the church and walked toward the waiting carriages.

"So very happy, my darling. Are you?"

Lottie beamed. "I could not be happier, Mama."

"I am certain we shall both be happier every day." She squeezed her daughter's hand as they parted, and Fitzwilliam assisted her into the carriage. She pressed against him, laying her head on his shoulder, and savored the moment. It was among the first of many with her new husband, and joy and contentment filled her.

PLEASE SIGN UP FOR Abbey's newsletter[1] to receive information about new releases. If you have any difficulties, email Abbey to request a manual add.

---

1. https://www.subscribepage.com/JAFF

About The Author

ABBEY IS A DIEHARD Jane Austen fan and has loved Fitzwilliam since the first time she "met" him at age thirteen upon borrowing the book from the school library. He is the ideal man, though Abbey's husband is a close second. Abbey enjoys writing various steamy and sweet Jane Austen variations, but "Pride & Prejudice" (and Mr. Darcy) will always be her favorite.

Did you love *Marrying Mr. Darcy: A Sensual "Pride & Prejudice" Variation*? Then you should read *Compromising Mr. Darcy: A Steamy "Pride & Prejudice" Variation*[1] by Abbey North!

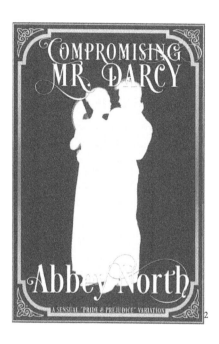

Mr. Darcy likes to be in control...

After a revealing midnight meeting in Netherfield's library, Lizzy can't keep her thoughts from Mr. Darcy. When her mother lies to her about Mr. Bennet's impending death to force her to marry Cousin Collins, she acts in hasty desperation and compromises Mr. Darcy with a kiss. He won't hear of her refusing his grudging proposal, both because he wants to preserve his honor and Georgiana's standing, and because he suspects Lizzy has certain tastes that will well-suit his

1. https://books2read.com/u/3Rz8eL

2. https://books2read.com/u/3Rz8eL

own proclivities. That doesn't keep him from being angry that she viewed him only as a choice moderately preferable to Mr. Collins, and the resentment seems impossible to overcome.

With his sister determined to dislike Lizzy and make her suffer for forcing him into marriage, and Fitzwilliam himself seemingly unable to forgive her, any attempt to be happy seems doomed. They entered marriage as adversaries, but can the passion growing between them help them find a new accord, or will Lizzy be forced to continue to for pay compromising Mr. Darcy?

While Abbey sometimes writes sweet JAFF, this is strictly SENSUAL. It has mild scenes of a dominant nature.

Also by Abbey North

Darcy's Courtesan
Adversity (Darcy's Courtesan, Part One)
Avidity (Darcy's Courtesan, Part Two)
Amity (Darcy's Courtesan, Part Three)
Darcy's Courtesan: A Sensual "Pride & Prejudice" Variation

Marriage & Mysteries
Honeymoon & Hemlock

Mr. Darcy's Secret Stories
Mistaken Masquerade: A Pride & Prejudice Variation
Mischief & Matchmaking: A "Pride & Prejudice" Variation

Standalone
Christmas At Pemberley: A Pride & Prejudice Variation
A Scandalous Proposition: A Pride & Prejudice Variation
Shadow of Darcy: A Sensual Pride & Prejudice Paranormal
Variation
Darcy's Obsession
Blackmailing Lizzy: A "Pride & Prejudice" Variation
Darcy's Wicked Game
Danger With Darcy: A Sensual "Pride & Prejudice" Variation
Passion & Prostrations: A Sensual "Pride & Prejudice" Variation
Darcy's Debt: A Sensual Pride & Prejudice Variation

Lightning Source UK Ltd.
Milton Keynes UK
UKHW010952080223
416610UK00015B/1807